DATE DUE

Library of Congress Cataloging-in-Publication Data

Cole, Joanna.
Who put the pepper in the pot?/by Joanna Cole;
pictures by Robert Alley.
p. cm.
Summary: Mama Sue, Papa Joe and the kids prepare
a fiery pot of stew for visiting Aunt Tootie.
ISBN 0-8193-1189-8
[1. Family life—Fiction.   2. Cookery—Fiction.]
I. Alley, R.W. (Robert W.), ill.   II. Title.
PZ7.C67346Wh   1989
[E]—dc19   88-36625
                                    CIP

A Parents Magazine
Read Aloud Original

WHO PUT THE PEPPER IN THE POT?

by Joanna Cole · pictures by R.W. Alley

PARENTS MAGAZINE PRESS · NEW YORK

Mama Sue and Papa Joe had a big old farm
all coming up weeds.
They had a little old house
all peeling off paint.
And they had a bunch of kids
all growing up faster than their clothes.
They lived on hard work
sweetened with love.

One day, a letter came.
Rich Aunt Tootie was coming
for dinner.

"Tootie's used to a fancy life,"
worried Papa Joe.
"What will she think of our poor place?"

"We may be poor,"
said Mama Sue.
"But we can cook up a hearty stew
as good as Tootie's ever tasted."

Everyone helped.
Papa Joe got the meat.
Sam chopped onions and potatoes.
Toby and Jane sliced carrots.
They put everything in the pot
with some water,
and Mama Sue put the pot on the fire.

Then Papa Joe said, "Now for the chores."
Everybody got to work.

Mama Sue was washing clothes on the porch
when she heard the stew say,
"Bubble, bubble!"
She remembered that
she had not put any pepper in the pot.
And how in the world can a stew be hearty
without pepper?

"Hey, Joe!"
Mama Sue called.
"Will you put some pepper in the pot?"

"I can't now, Sue,"
called Joe from the wood pile.
"I'm chopping wood."

"Oh, fiddle!"
said Mama Sue.

"Bubble, bubble!"
said the stew, a little louder.

"Hey, Sam!"
called Mama Sue.
"Will you put some pepper in the pot?"

"I can't, Ma,"
yelled Sam from the front porch.
"I'm polishing windows."

"Oh, faddle!"
said Mama Sue.

"Bubble, bubble!"
said the stew, even louder.

"Toby! Jane!"
called Mama Sue.
"Will you put some pepper in the pot?"

"We can't now, Ma,"
yelled Toby and Jane from the yard.
"We're cutting grass."

"Oh, twiddle,"
said Mama Sue,
but she was all in soapsuds
up to her elbows,
so *she* couldn't put the pepper in the pot.

"Bubble-bubble-bubble,"
grumbled the stew.

A little later,
Papa Joe said to himself,
"I'm finished chopping.
I'd better put that pepper in the pot."

He went to the kitchen
and put in a pinch of pepper.

A little later,
Sam said to himself,
"I'm finished polishing.
I'll put the pepper in the pot."

He went to the kitchen
and put in *two* pinches.

A little later,
Toby and Jane said,
"We're finished cutting.
Let's put the pepper in the pot."

They went to the kitchen
and put in *three* pinches.

A little later,
Mama Sue said to herself,
"I asked everyone to put in pepper,
and everyone said no.
I'd better do it myself.
It's a big stew, so I'll put in extra."

She went to the kitchen
and put *four* pinches
of pepper in the pot.
"*That* will make it hearty,"
said Mama Sue.

By dinner time,
the clothes were clean,
the grass was cut,
the wood was chopped,
the windows were shiny,
and the stew smelled mighty hearty.

And in came Aunt Tootie,
all dressed up and hungry as a bear.
They kissed her hello.
They gave her the best chair.
They gave her the plate without the crack.
And Mama Sue dished out the stew.

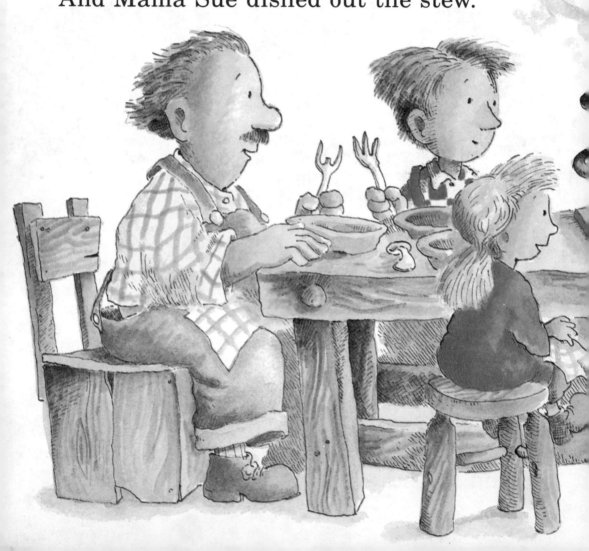

To be polite, everyone waited
for Aunt Tootie to begin first.
She lifted her fork,
took a bite,

and, oh, what a face she made!

She breathed some air,
she drank some water,
and she shed some tears.
Then she looked around the table.

"WHO put the pepper in the pot?"
she roared.

Everyone answered at once.
"*I* put the pepper in the pot!"
said Mama Sue and Papa Joe
and Sam and Toby and Jane.

They all took a bite.
"Yeeooow!!"
They looked at Tootie's face.
She was frowning,
but Toby and Jane saw
a little smile trying to peek through.
Then a little giggle came out,
and a bigger giggle,
and then a great *haw-haw-haw*!
Pretty soon, everyone was laughing.

"We can't eat that stew,"
said Papa Joe.

"Let's make something else,"
said Mama Sue.

"We'll make my famous omelet—
Eggs Supreme,"
said Aunt Tootie.

Tootie took off her shoes.
She put on an apron.
She called for eggs.
She called for onions.
She called for parsley.
She called for basil, tomatoes,
salt, and pepper.

"What?"
"Pepper?"
"Sorry, Aunt Tootie!"

There wasn't a pinch of pepper
left in the whole house.
Thank goodness!

About the Author

Joanna Cole can't imagine how Mama Sue and Papa Joe can stand the way they cook. "I recently got a microwave," she says. "Now that I've used it, I would hate to try cooking with a giant pot over a fire!"

Ms. Cole has written many books for children, including the *Clown-Around* books for Parents. She lives in New York with her husband and daughter.

About the Illustrator

Robert Alley based this story's setting on what was formerly his great-great-grandparents' tobacco plantation, which he once visited. "When I saw the house, it was so old, tired, and ramshackle that even Sue and Joe's family couldn't help it!"

Mr. Alley also wrote and illustrated *The Ghost In Dobbs Diner* for Parents. He and his wife live in Rhode Island.